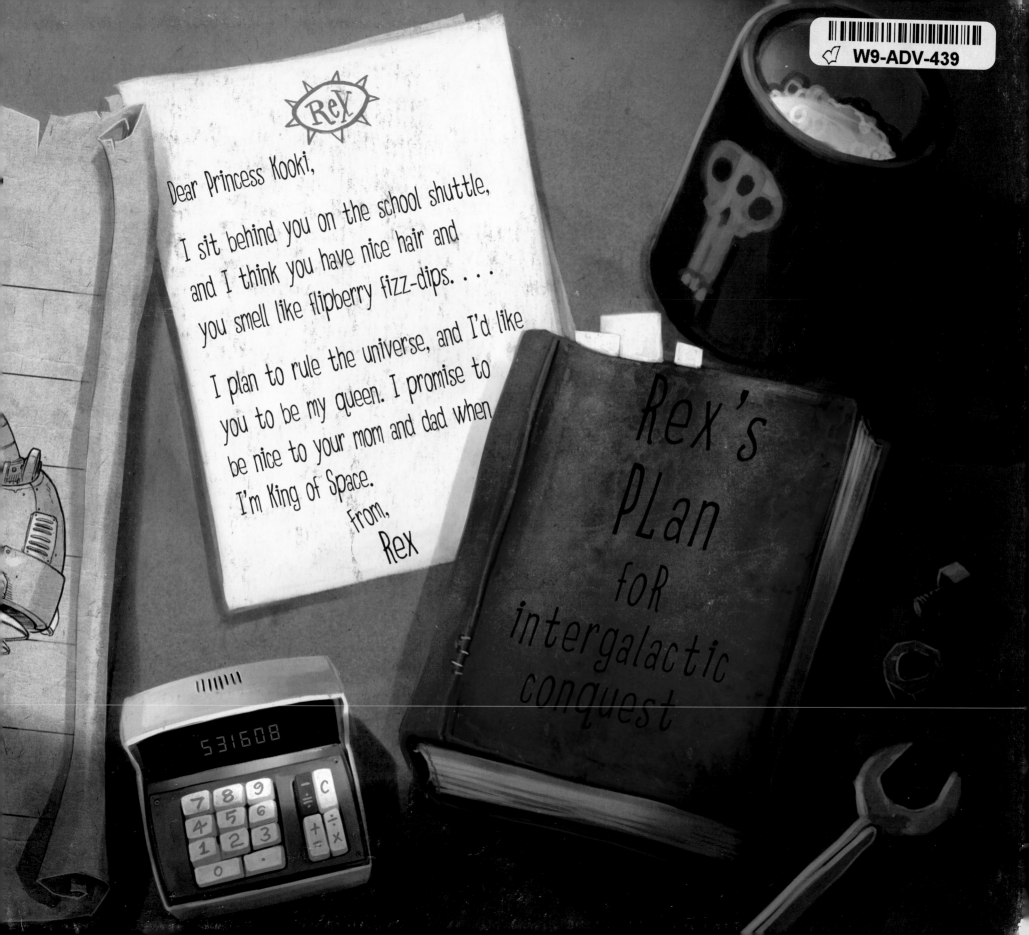

Dear Princess Kooki,

I sit behind you on the school shuttle, and I think you have nice hair and you smell like flipberry fizz-dips. . . .

I plan to rule the universe, and I'd like you to be my queen. I promise to be nice to your mom and dad when I'm King of Space.

From,

Rex

Rex's Plan for intergalactic conquest

531608

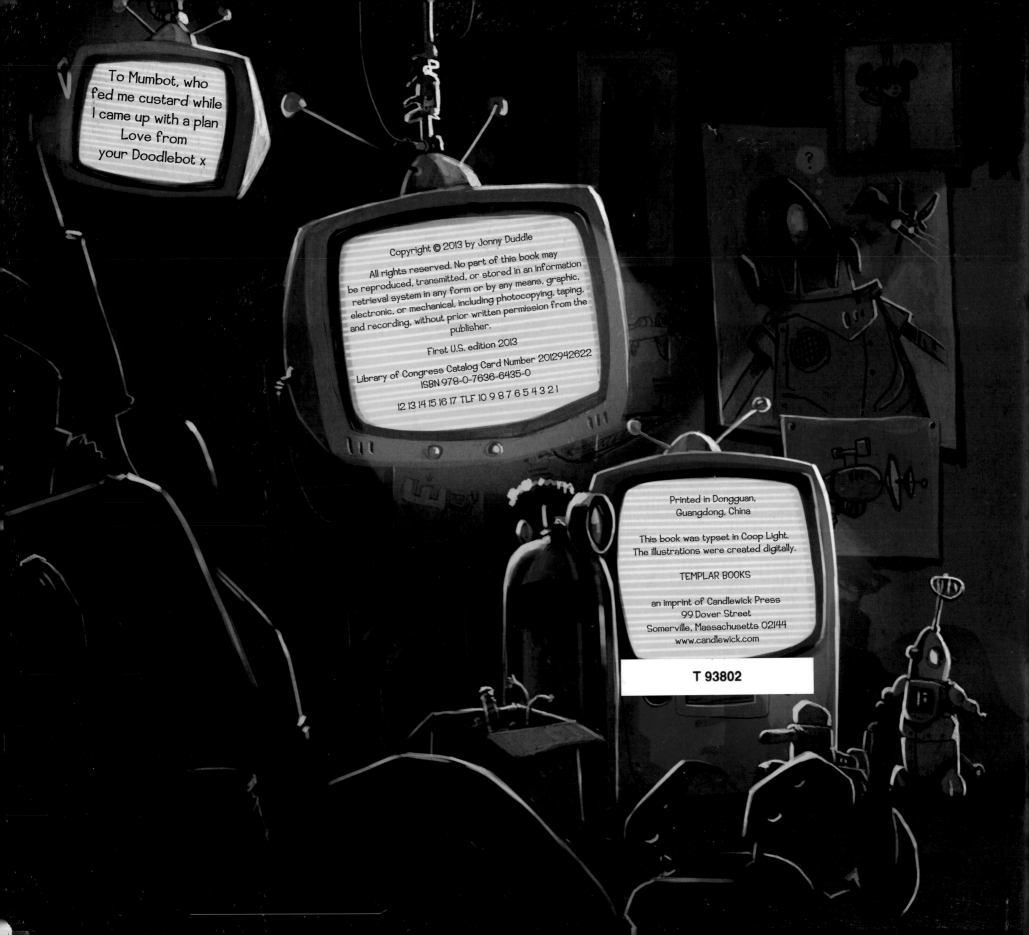

To Mumbot, who
fed me custard while
I came up with a plan
Love from
your Doodlebot x

First U.S. edition 2013

Library of Congress Catalog Card Number 2012942622
ISBN 978-0-7636-6435-0

12 13 14 15 16 17 TLF 10 9 8 7 6 5 4 3 2 1

Printed in Dongguan,
Guangdong, China

This book was typset in Coop Light.
The illustrations were created digitally.

TEMPLAR BOOKS

an imprint of Candlewick Press
99 Dover Street
Somerville, Massachusetts 02144
www.candlewick.com

THE KING OF SPACE

SOON THE WHOLE UNIVERSE WILL KNOW MY NAME!

Jonny Duddle

Mom and Dad say I have too much energy, so they have to keep me busy.

But on this particular night, I was too busy to clean my room.

I'd just thought up my BIGGEST and BESTEST PLAN EVER!

I'M GOING TO FLY SPACE FREIGHTERS. VROOOOOM!

ERM . . . IT'D BE REALLY NICE TO FIX DRAINS LIKE MY DAD.

I JUST WANNA MAKE COMPUTER GAMES, DUDE!

YES, MA'AM. I'M TRAINING TO BE A SPACE MARINE, MA'AM!

WELL, MISS BRAIN . . .

I'VE DEVELOPED A CLEVER PLAN . . .

A PLAN TO TAKE ME FROM THIS LOWLY CLASSROOM TO THE FARTHEST REACHES OF SPACE!

I WILL BE THE **KING** OF **SPACE!**

I WILL CREATE AN ARMY SO POWERFUL THAT ONLY THE MOST FOOLISH WILL DARE TO STAND AGAINST ME!

I WILL CRUSH PLANETS AND SQUISH SOLAR SYSTEMS!

SOON THE WHOLE UNIVERSE WILL KNOW MY NAME. . . .

For homework that night, Miss Brain asked us to each build a robot that could do something helpful.

Miss Brain said she was very impressed with everybody else's robots . . .

Blip's spaceship-washbot,

Xarg's toast-o-matic (with net),

Zorick's lawn-mowing-machine,

and even Glob's drain-unblocking-droid.

Miss Brain asked my mom and dad to come into school.

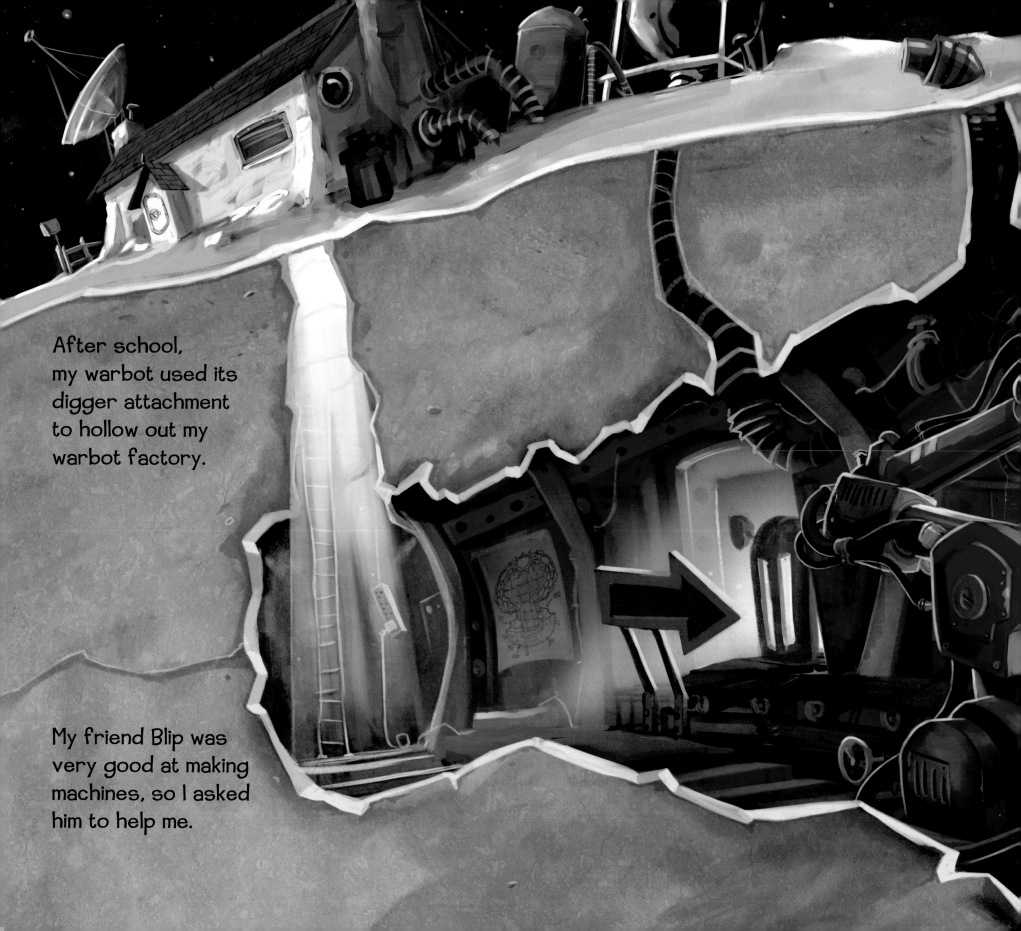

After school, my warbot used its digger attachment to hollow out my warbot factory.

My friend Blip was very good at making machines, so I asked him to help me.

He agreed, but only after I promised that it was part of an extra-credit assignment.

MY VERY OWN PLANET?

REEEEEALLY?

YES.

AND I COULD DO WHATEVER I LIKE THERE?

UM . . .

YES.

I COULD STAY UP LATE AND WATCH TV AND EAT **LOTS** OF CHOCOLATE?

ON YOUR PLANET, YOU'D BE **ALL-POWERFUL!**

WOW!

WOULD I STILL HAVE TO CLEAN MY ROOM?

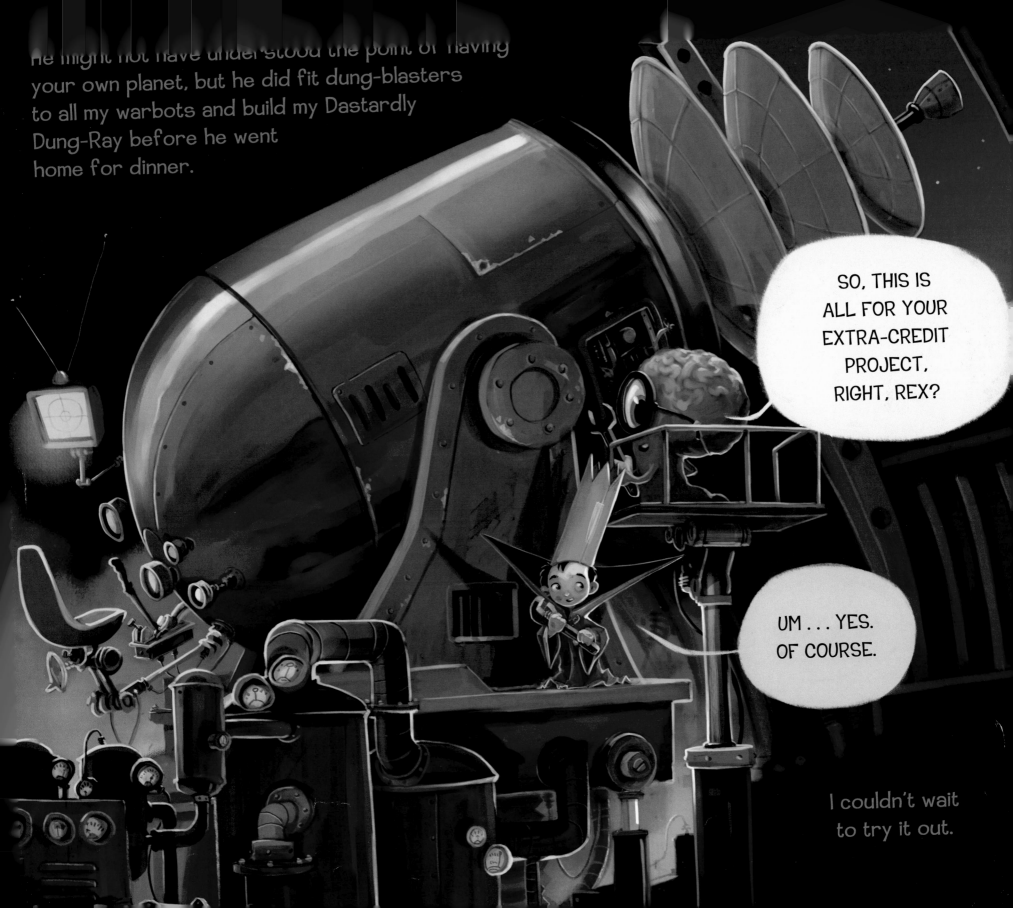

After my victory,
I decided it was time
for my CORONATION!

I handed out invitations
to all my friends at school
and made everyone
promise that they
wouldn't tell their
moms and dads.

Blip even created a direct feed so that
everyone in the universe had to watch my coronation ceremony—
whether they liked it or not.

REX

I NOW
CROWN MYSELF
THE **KING** OF
SPACE!

**CLAP
NOW!**

I gave
a moon to
everyone who
clapped a lot.

I tried to sneak past Mom and Dad to get the choco-goo.
There was lots of great stuff on the news about my warbots taking over
the universe and Princess Kooki being held hostage.

BREAKING NEWS'   GALACTIC ALLIANCE SEARCHING FOR "KING OF SPACE" • NOW IN SMELL-O-VISION!

OOOH, REX —
YOU LOOK JUST
LIKE THE EVIL
LEADER OF THE
INVASION FLEET!

UM . . .
DO I?

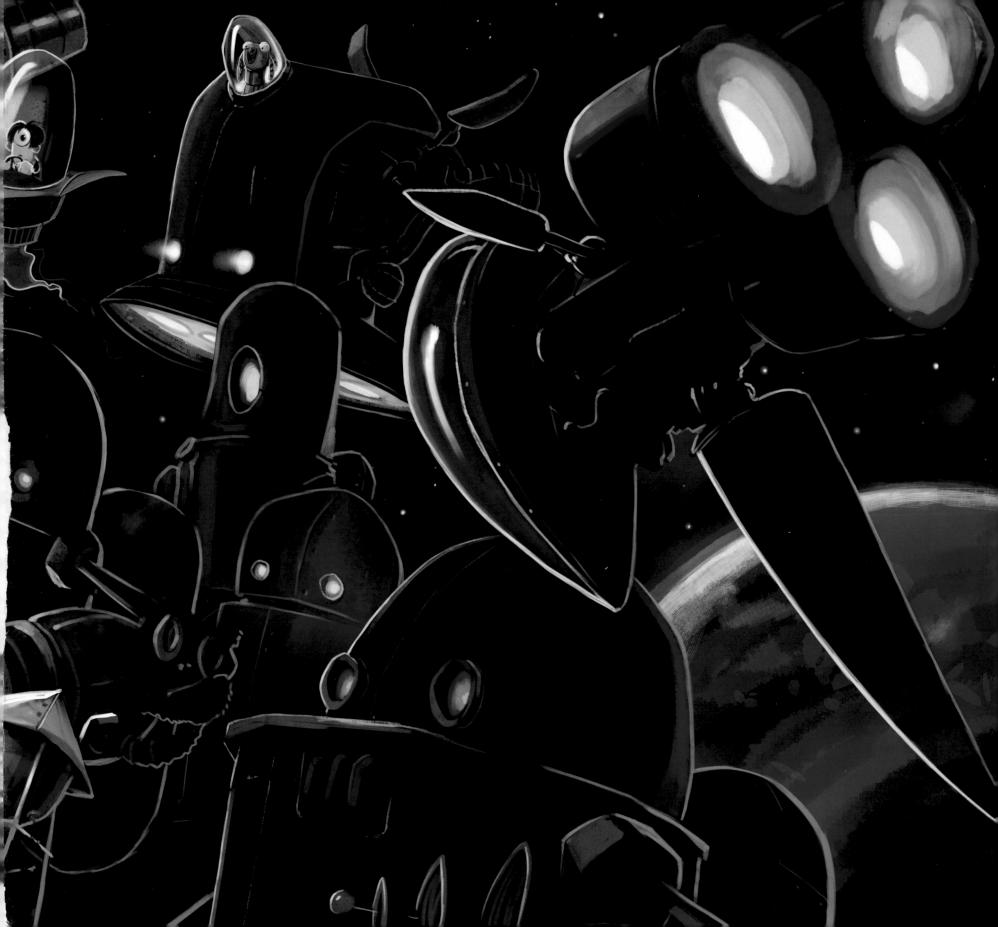

I ran inside and slammed the door.

WHAT'S WRONG, REX?

I ... ER ... UM ... THEY ... ERM ...

COME ON, SPIT IT OUT HONEY!

WELL, THE GALACTIC ALLIANCE IS OUTSIDE, AND THEY'RE REALLY MAD BECAUSE I INVADED THEIR PLANETS, KIDNAPPED PRINCESS KOOKI, AND CROWNED MYSELF ...

THE KING OF SPACE.

THE WHAT?

THE KING OF SPACE.

AND I REALLY AM!

Then I told Mom and Dad everything I'd been up to.

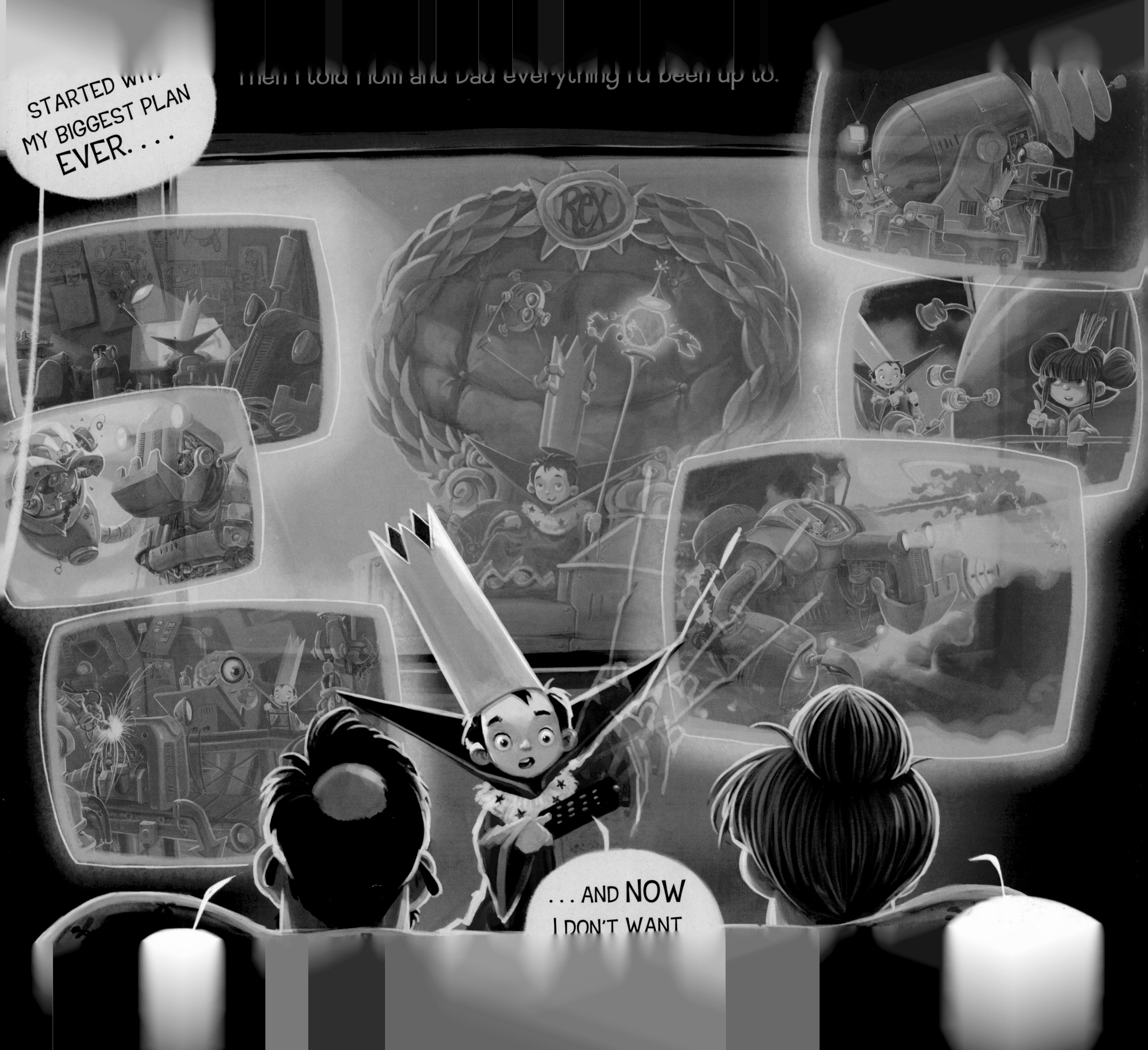

Luckily, even the Galactic Alliance is a little afraid of Mom, so they took Princess Kooki back and went home. Then Dad made me some hot chocolate, helped me brush my teeth, and read me a bedtime story.

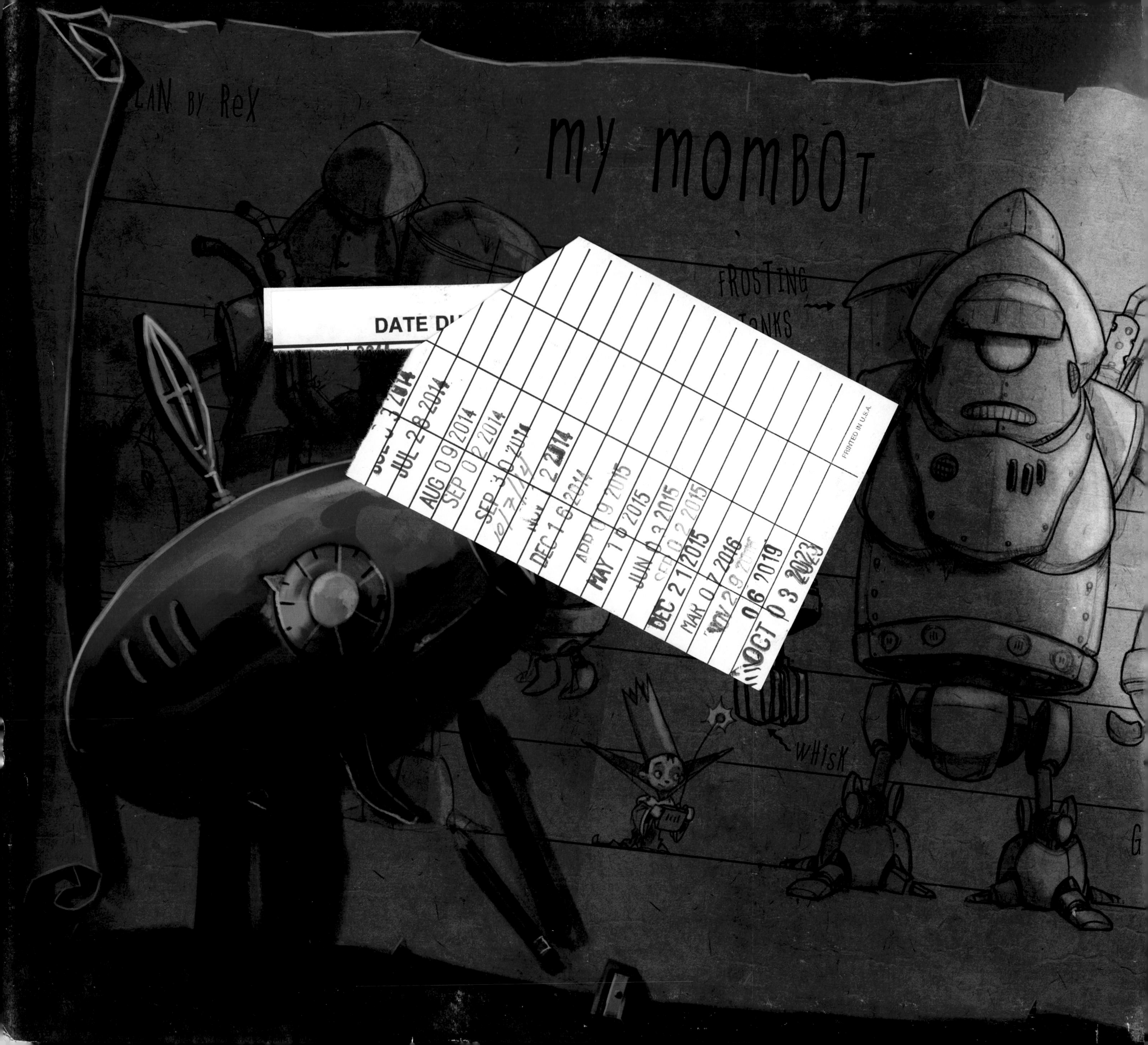
LAN BY ReX
my mombot
FROSTING TANKS
WHisk